Books

Down the Pier

'walk down the pier, a walk down the pier,' Davy
nself as he shivered. Everything was roaring with
verything black and wet and hissing and splash-
blew through his thin sweater as he stood there,
in the little pool of yellow from the light behind

anded at the end of the rain-lashed pier, with his
d Mr Pennyquick lying unconscious from a fall,
had to walk down the pier to the town for help.
could Davy brave a walk that would have been
y in daytime but was now a nightmare of hidden
gers as the rickety pier was rocked and shaken by
sea? Or was there another way to get help?
Davy's danger and his determination to help his
iend will keep all readers of six and over on the edge of
eir seats.

and brought up in Frome,
clerk, then a publicity assist-
ce agent, which he still is. He
d is married with grown-up

D1421634

Other books by John Escott
BURGLAR BELLS
RADIO ALERT
RADIO DETECTIVE
RADIO REPORTERS
RADIO RESCUE

Illustrated by Frances Phillips

John Escott

A Walk Down the Pier

Puffin Books

PUFFIN BOOKS

Published by the Penguin Group
27 Wrights Lane, London w8 5tz, England
Viking Penguin Inc., 375 Hudson Street, New York, New York 10014, USA
Penguin Books Australia Ltd, Ringwood, Victoria, Australia
Penguin Books Canada Ltd, 2801 John Street, Markham, Ontario, Canada l3r 1b4
Penguin Books (NZ) Ltd, 182–190 Wairau Road, Auckland 10, New Zealand

Penguin Books Ltd, Registered Offices: Harmondsworth, Middlesex, England

First published by Hamish Hamilton Children's Books 1977
Published in Puffin Books 1981
10 9 8 7

Printed in England by Clays Ltd, St Ives plc
Set in Monotype Baskerville

. I

Mr Pennyquick's tongue crept stealthily out of the corner of his mouth as he flicked the merest touch of grey paint into the middle of the skull of the skeleton. The great hollow eye-sockets and laughing mouth stared back at him but Mr Pennyquick did not flinch. He had painted many skeletons in his lifetime – skeletons, monsters, ghosts, dragons.

It was the dragons that Davy liked best. They were the subject of his own paintings very often Huge green dragons which breathed fire and smoke and flew through the sky licking the tree-tops with their tongues of flame.

Davy painted on almost any flat surface going. The pictures were always a bit fantastic,

painted in a frenzy of excitement with bright sploshy strokes and no thought at all about the way things really looked. Davy's own versions were always much more satisfying to him.

Now, watching the old signwriter high up on the tallest pair of steps Davy had ever seen, he marvelled at the realness of the skeleton. Almost as though it might climb down from the top of the booth and put its bony arms around you.

Davy shuddered.

Mr Pennyquick climbed down the steps, the clatter of his feet echoing round the empty building. Empty and silent as though some wizard had cast a spell on all the occupants except Davy and the old man with the paint-brush.

The horses on the roundabout stood frozen in their circle; silent, grinning faces staring into space. The bumper cars huddled together in one corner of their circuit awaiting drivers and power to send them sparking and crackling on their way. The carriages of the Treasure Trail

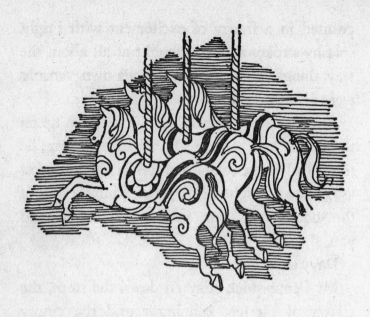

Train stood in an orderly line along one wall, its engine gone for repairs.

Mr Pennyquick dragged the huge pair of steps further along the front of the booth where the ghost train sat waiting.

'All right, Davy? Not bored, are you?'

Davy shook his head. There was only one thing better than watching Mr Pennyquick and that was doing a painting yourself.

'You'll be giving me a hand soon,' the old

man said as he reclimbed the steps, 'the way your painting is improving.'

He began to touch up the lettering which read: SCREAMS! THRILLS! THE SPOOKIEST THING ON THE PIER!

Davy looked round the brightly lit hall. Not so bright as when the funfair was in full swing, of course. When lights flashed brilliant colours and people shrieked and shouted with delight. He had never seen it like that, being quite new to the town. He had arrived with his parents just after Christmas and at first had felt lonely and out of things.

Then he had met Mr Pennyquick.

The signwriter had come to do the board which was fixed to his father's car, the one which told people his Dad was a driving instructor. Davy had been painting on a sheet of cardboard in the corner of the kitchen while Mr Pennyquick and his Dad had been discussing the new sign. The old man stole frequent glances at the work going on in the corner and eventually came across for a closer inspection. Davy was embarrassed. His pictures belonged strictly to his own private world and he hated having to discuss them with anybody.

Mr Pennyquick had stood for a full minute before he murmured, 'Hm. Well that's certainly one way of looking at it,' and shuffled out of the house.

The next time he had come he had a suggestion.

'I've some old signs and pieces of board you might find useful for your paintings, Davy. Come round and take a look.'

And that was the beginning of a very special friendship for Davy. Mr Pennyquick gave him a corner of his workshop to use as his 'studio' and supplied him with odds and ends of paint and brushes together with advice and encouragement.

Mind you, it meant putting up with Mr Pennyquick's granddaughter occasionally. Davy always felt uncomfortable when she was around. Not that she ever said anything unkind

or rude, but she managed to make it clear she thought Davy a bit of a wet weakling.

'Meg thinks everybody should be as briskly efficient as herself,' Mr Pennyquick explained. 'Yet really she's as warm-hearted a soul as you'd wish to meet.'

But in the few short weeks he had known Mr Pennyquick, Davy had never seen her anything but aloof and snooty.

He had gone on several jobs with the old man

since the start of the Easter holidays, just to watch and to listen to Mr Pennyquick explaining what he was doing. Then came the pier job. Normally, Mr Pennyquick had explained, this would have been done earlier in the year during the daytime, but there had been so much other work to do, so many signs to paint and touch up, he had just not found the time. Then the man from the council had come, Mr Bragg, or whatever his name was.

'We could get somebody else in to touch up the paintwork on the booths and things, if you're too busy, Mr Pennyquick. I expect you find it a bit of a strain these days . . .'

Even Davy had recognized the threat in the cocky little man's words. Too old, they thought Mr Pennyquick. Too tired, not able to cope. He had seen the hurt look on the old man's face as he had quickly assured Mr Bragg that the work would be done in time for the opening of the funfair at Easter.

So, after they had finished the job at the Chinese Take-Away earlier that afternoon,

Davy and Mr Pennyquick had come along the pier to the funfair.

Now the old man was on the final sign above the booth of the ghost train and Davy noticed how tired he looked. Outside the hall the rain beat down in the darkness, whipping up the grey sea and soaking the planked flooring and polished rail of the old pier. The wind was getting up as it often did at the end of March and Davy felt the framework creak and sway slightly.

Inside, listening, he felt snug and protected. He imagined the blackness outside and was glad he had brought his anorak. He was glad too that he would have the comforting, reassuring presence of Mr Pennyquick when the time came to retrace their steps back along the pier. The moon would be hidden behind the dark clouds and they would need the light of the powerful torch Mr Pennyquick had stuffed in his back pocket.

'Nearly finished now,' the old man called down, painting the large blob at the bottom of the exclamation mark. 'You'll be wanting your supper, I expect. Your Mum know where you are?'

'She knows I'm with you,' Davy answered. He began gathering up the paintpots and bits of rag and sandpaper, putting them into the wooden box Mr Pennyquick carried with him when he went out on a job.

Above him, Mr Pennyquick tucked his brush into the breast-pocket of his overall and rubbed his tired eyes behind the spectacles.

'That's it then,' he said, resting the tin of paint on the platform of the steps and casting a critical eye along the length of the booth. It seemed to meet with his approval and, after wiping his fingers with a rag, he stooped and reached for the paint tin. Just for a moment everything blurred, then it cleared again leaving Mr Pennyquick feeling slightly faint. He stood for a moment then began to climb down.

'Are you all right, Mr Pennyquick?' Davy's sharp eyes had spotted the old man's pause as he had bent over the tin of paint.

'It's nothing. Just felt a little dizzy for a moment.'

It was as though Davy had a forewarning about the accident, like a flash of light, a picture on a screen in his head. Anyway, he had already begun to shout 'Be careful' when it happened.

The old man was half-way down when he missed his footing. He made a grab for the side of the steps, dropping the tin of paint which ended up splattered underneath him. His hand missed and the sudden jerk was enough to topple the stepladder itself.

Davy watched, his eyes wide, as the old man crashed down. He landed on his feet but immediately toppled over backwards, cracking his head on the wooden floor. Then he lay still.

. 2

Meg was perched on a high stool in the corner of the kitchen. It was hot and steamy in the tiny room and the rain beat against the window at her side.

'Grandad will get wet when he comes up from the workshop,' she stated briskly. 'I'll pop down soon with the umbrella.'

Her mother, an older, tireder version of Meg, was pushing an iron back and forth along the collar of a check workshirt of her father's. The wooden table in the centre of the kitchen which would later bear the old man's supper was now doubling as an ironing board. She looked up wearily and stared at the window.

'I certainly don't want him catching cold again, not with that chest of his. I can't make

him see it but what your grandfather needs is a good long rest. It's time he took things easier.'

Meg nodded, absently drawing the outline of an elephant on the misted window. Then she rubbed it away making a clear patch through which she could watch the rain. She worried about her grandad, too, but knew he was tougher than he looked. Sometimes she marvelled at his strength as he carried a large, heavy sign down from his workshop single-handed, then tossed it into the back of his van or lifted it on to the roof-rack with practised ease.

'My Mam fed me on nuts and bolts,' he would say with a huge wink, 'so I've iron arms.'

Even so, Meg had noticed he was slowing down just lately.

'I suppose he will be at the workshop and not out on some job,' her mother said as she examined a frayed cuff on the shirt.

'His van was outside there when I went by earlier this afternoon,' Meg said. 'I expect he's there. Anyway, he has to come back to park the van and then walk home so he'll need the umbrella.'

Which was true. Mr Pennyquick's workshop was over the top of two lock-up garages, one of which he used for his van. That left a walk up the steep, narrow hill to his house. The house where his daughter and grand-daughter lived with him.

It was tucked away at the top of the little seaside town, above the main shopping streets. Narrow, twisting terraces snaked upwards between workshops and warehouses, and houses with tiny squares of garden front and back. It was well away from where the holidaymakers congregated in the summer, except for those who liked to stray a little and see what went on behind the scenes.

Meg took off her glasses and cleaned a smudge from them with the corner of her handkerchief. Then, seeing the state of the handkerchief itself, hastily stuffed it back into the pocket of her jeans before her mother caught sight of it.

'One thing,' her mother was saying, 'that

young Davy has been a help to Grandad. Saves the old chap's legs no end, fetching and carrying things for him. He's a nice lad.'

Meg sniffed and said nothing. It wasn't that she did not like Davy. After all, he never said enough to make you like *or* dislike him.

Her mother had noticed her silence and looked up. 'You do like Davy, don't you, dear?'

'He's such a *dream*,' complained Meg. 'Most of the boys at school think he is wet. Except Melvin, and he would like almost anybody.'

'Davy's just a quiet one,' her mother said. 'Your Grandad says there's more to Davy than meets the eye. And as for his painting –'

'Oh, those *paintings*,' broke in Meg. 'Every one is a – a mini nightmare! Real scary – weird.'

'Grandad says it shows imagination,' her mother went on, refusing for once to have her mind changed by her headstrong daughter. She deftly changed the subject before the argument could be pursued further. 'By the way, I shall have to go on a bit earlier tonight. I've to drop in and see old Mrs Sherwood on my way to the hospital. I'd take the umbrella down myself but I shan't be passing the workshop tonight.' She looked at the window again. 'And just listen to that rain.'

Meg's mother worked as a night-nurse at the hospital most nights in the week. She enjoyed seeing to things for people unable to do anything for themselves. It made her feel important, something she rarely felt at home where she was swamped by the forceful characters of her father and daughter. And often she would call in on somebody on the way to the hospital. Somebody like Mrs Sherwood who had been in hospital herself until recently and was still not able to get about.

Meg slid off the stool. 'Hm, well perhaps you had better leave a meat pie for me to heat through in the oven,' she said. 'Grandad likes those pies from the corner shop.'

'Yes dear, that's just what I had thought of doing.' Her mother sighed. Sometimes, for a ten-year-old, Meg seemed to be terribly grown-up. She seemed to be getting away from her, out of reach. She looked at the clock. 'Well, I'll have to go, and it's time you did, otherwise Grandad will be leaving the workshop before you get down there. If he does he'll be soaked in no time.'

Meg heard the rain as she pulled on her boots and mac. Then she watched her mother disappear up the hill towards the church before setting off in the opposite direction.

She opened Grandad's large, black umbrella which he hardly ever used, but once outside the wind was so strong she nearly took off like Mary Poppins. In the end Meg decided it would be safer to do without on the way down and then let Grandad cope with it coming back. However, it meant she became drenched in the short distance down the hill to the workshop.

When she reached the little vard in front of the two garages a disappointment awaited her. Grandad's van was not there and the workshop above was in darkness.

'Blow,' Meg said to herself.

The door to the workshop was at the top of an

iron spiral staircase which curled up the side of the building. The light from the street was barely enough to show her the way but Meg made the slippery climb. She decided she might as well wait in the dry until the van returned. Perhaps Grandad was taking Davy home first. Yes, that was it, she decided. It wouldn't do for poor Master Davy to get his feet wet, now would it?

Grandad kept a spare key on a hook underneath the top step and Meg fumbled about in the darkness until she found it, then she unlocked the creaky door and stepped in, making a pool of rainwater just inside as she shut out the storm.

The workshop smelled of wood and paint and methylated spirit, and at first sight a person could be forgiven for thinking they had stumbled into a giant's reading room. Large signs and notice-boards with letters knee-high lay around the walls. Some were very old, the lettering cracked and peeling, others were sleekly new and modern in style.

Grandad's workbench was covered with drawings and sketches of signs and posters and the shelves above were cluttered with empty paint tins, jars, glue and old rags by the dozen.

'How does he find anything?' Meg said to herself. Several times she had tried to organize things for him but somehow it had always managed to slip back into Grandad's comfortable muddle.

In one corner of the workshop there was an area slightly less chaotic. This was Davy's 'studio'. The current masterpiece sat on a home-made easel in the centre, surrounded by neat piles of other pictures. Meg peered at the painting and screwed up her nose. It was of a giant jelly-fish, long trailing tentacles coming out from under its pinky, feathery dome. Davy had seen one on the beach a few days earlier and it had grown in his imagination taking on an eerie, menacing form.

All Davy's pictures were like that. Meg looked through some of the completed ones. A tiny tiger being chased by giant hedgehogs; a

scary dragon pursued by monster birds. Meg had watched him splashing on the paint and thought it was as though he was on another planet. He worked in a little world with everything else shut out.

She found the oil-stove and some matches and, taking great care, lit it the way she had seen Grandad do it. Then, climbing on to his high work stool, she pulled off her wet boots and settled down to wait.

'He won't be long,' she told herself.

·3

At first Davy thought he was going to be sick.
He seemed unable to move his feet from the
spot where he had stood watching the fall. They
were stuck to the floorboards with super-glue
and weighted down with lumps of lead, and
anyway, his eyes were closed now and he did
not want to open them up for a hundred years.
But he knew he had to and perhaps, if he did, he
would find everything all right again.

He blinked them open fiercely and stared.

Mr Pennyquick was lying there, his chest
jerkily rising and falling. Mr Pennyquick – hurt.
Mr Pennyquick, his friend. Mr Pennyquick,
who always seemed to know what Davy was
thinking but didn't like to say. Mr Pennyquick
who had helped him with his paintings, full of

suggestions and useful advice without actually interfering with Davy's own ideas. Helped him in dozens of ways, most of all by just being there to talk to.

And now Mr Pennyquick needed help. Needed it badly. And there was only Davy – alone.

He forced himself to go over to the still figure lying beside the fallen ladder.

'Mr Pennyquick.' His voice sounded miles away, a croak, but it didn't matter. Mr Pennyquick could not hear, he could see that.

The silence was even greater now, the scrape of his foot as he knelt beside the old man echoing around him. The painted face of the skeleton laughed mockingly down at him. 'You see,' it seemed to say, 'you see what happens when you tamper with us?' But the only real noise was the noise of the storm outside.

Shaking himself into action, Davy stood up and looked around. He had to make Mr Pennyquick more comfortable, he looked so awkward just lying there. Anyway, wasn't there something about keeping a person warm after an accident? His mother had said something that time their neighbour had slipped in the snow. They had brought her in and wrapped a blanket round her and given her some brandy in a glass. Though perhaps that was just because it was freezing cold and February then. Anyway, the funfair did not come equipped with brandy or blankets so that was no good.

Still, he had to do *something*.

There was a circular booth with a cone-shaped roof near the door. NON-STOP BINGO it said round the outside, and there were stools for people to sit on and lights which would flash on and off. The centre of the stand was draped with a large dust sheet. Davy clambered over the side and dragged it off. It wasn't a blanket but it would do. Climbing back, he bundled it up and struggled over to Mr Pennyquick. It was heavy and as much as he could carry but he managed to spread it carefully over the old man folding it two or three times until it lay quite thickly about him.

Next he looked round for something to act as a pillow. The floor was hard and dirty and Mr Pennyquick's cheek was resting in some of the spilled paint from the fallen paint tin. But there was nothing to be had and in the end Davy used his anorak folded over. With much difficulty he eased it under the old man's head.

Afterwards he stood up and looked to see if there was anything else he could do but there did not seem to be. Outside he could hear the wind was blowing much harder now and the sea pounding the sides of the pier.

He realized what he had to do and shuddered. He imagined the long, black, rain-soaking walk ahead of him. A walk without the comforting presence of Mr Pennyquick, without the large warm hand to grasp if the wind was rough, as it was.

'It's just a walk down the pier,' he told himself.

Then his heart stopped as he remembered the torch. The large, powerful light which was to have shown the way back. It was in the old man's pocket still.

Shaking and blinking back tears which had no business being in his eyes, Davy bent down and fumbled under the thickness of the dust sheet, his fingers groping under the heavy figure. Then he realized he was on the wrong side and stepped across, stumbling and almost falling. Stifling a sob he tried again and this time touched the glass of the torch. It was sharp and he drew his hand back with a cry of pain and licked the trickle of blood running over his fingernail.

The glass on the torch was smashed which probably meant the wretched thing no longer worked. But it had to work, it just *had* to.

But it didn't.

Having pulled it out, Davy flicked the switch back and forth at least a dozen times. Then he dropped the useless object to the floor and stared up at the high ceiling, almost as though an answer to all his problems might be written there – clearly, in giant-sized letters specially painted by Mr Pennyquick at some time just in case this sort of thing happened.

Then he looked at the big blue exit doors and knew he would have to go now. Quickly, before he had too much time to think about how terrible it was going to be walking out there in the darkness, without even a torch.

At least Mr Pennyquick looked comfortable now, still breathing jerkily, but comfortable. At the blue doors he looked back just once before heaving one of them open.

First there was the noise of the sea crashing on the pier supports, then there was the wind which blew Davy backwards. He staggered out again looking into the darkness. He could not see the end of the pier from where he stood although he could make out the lights of the town beyond.

Mellisea was built on a hill. A jumble of buildings piled one above the other like an untidy heap of odd-shaped parcels. A square-towered church topped the pile, a protective parent shielding the whole town from the noisy bypass which ran behind it. But now it was just smears of orange light blinking dimly through the blackness of the rain.

Davy slid out of the door and was engulfed by the noise. Everything roaring with wind. Everything black and wet and hissing and splashing. It blew through his thin sweater as he stood there, frozen in the little pool of yellow from the light behind him.

'Just a walk down the pier, a walk down the pier,' he told himself as he shivered.

He wished he had his anorak. But then, if he was going to start wishing he might as well wish for something worthwhile. Like a torch. Like somebody coming out of the darkness to help him. Like closing his eyes and turning the clock back and not having this happen at all.

The rain splattered over him, chilling his bones until he felt like the skeleton Mr Pennyquick had been painting, shaking and exposed. The wet got in his eyes and down his shirt and into his shoes. It plastered his hair down round his collar and over his face.

Still he did not move. Outside the pool of light was no-man's-land. Different to the daylight when it was just a walk down the pier with deckchairs and people fishing.

'You certainly have an imagination, Davy,' Mr Pennyquick had said often.

'Those pictures of yours – all nightmares and creepy crawlies,' Meg had said.

Too much imagination, Davy thought. Like now, when the pier wasn't a pier any more but a dark tunnel with fingers reaching out as you walked and noises and splashing and . . .

Davy shut his eyes. This was no good. He had to close his mind up, put the lid down and sit on it – at least until he reached the other end of the pier. Come on, feet – *move*. Out of the yellow and into the black and don't stop!

It was difficult to know where to walk. In the centre of the pier the wind buffeted him until he could hardly stand. Without anything to hold on to he began losing his sense of direction. Was he still going forwards or sideways?

Somehow he found his way over to the rail at

the side. It was better at first, moving hand over
hand, but then the sea splashed up over his feet
and legs and he became frightened he would be
washed over the side.

He looked back to the light from the doors of
the funfair. How far had he come, ten, twenty
miles? It seemed at least that far but the light
told him different, he was barely half-way.

Then he heard the crash.

It was a great tearing, splintering, ripping
noise and the whole pier seemed to move under
some tremendous impact. Then, just ahead of
him, Davy saw a great chunk of flooring break

and drop downwards into a boiling sea. The rail on his side of the pier snapped off and hung like a broken arm.

Davy cried out and sank to the floor. For the second time that evening he was unable to make himself move.

· 4

Meg walked over to the window above the yard and looked down. There was still no sign of Grandad or his van, just the watery yellow eye of the street lamp and rain, rain, rain.

Away to her right across the rooftops was the sea but Meg's eyes were on the empty yard.

'Where *is* he?'

She looked at the old alarm clock on the shelf above the bench. He should have been back ages ago. She stamped back over to the oil-stove and warmed her hands, cross and slightly worried. He would know her mother would have left for the hospital by now and he always made a point of being back by then. Of course he had not known she was leaving early that evening to visit Mrs Sherwood, but even so . . .

Meg tried to remember if he had said what he was working on. Her grandfather liked to talk about what he was doing, usually at mealtimes. She tried to remember what he had said at breakfast. Something – something about dragons. That was it, the dragon at the Chinese Take-Away. He had laughed about it saying how Davy would enjoy watching his favourite monster being painted. Could he still be there now?

'Well, finding out is better than sitting about here,' Meg said to herself.

She turned off the stove and pulled on her boots, glad to be leaving the empty workshop and its silence.

She had squelched half-way down the hill before it occurred to her she could have used the telephone at the workshop. Although she did not know the number of the Take-Away, and finding a telephone directory amongst Grandad's clutter would have meant a treasure-hunt. Soggily, she trudged on down, her head bent against the driving rain.

The Dragon's Tooth Chinese Take-Away served hot Chinese meals to take home or, if you preferred, at tables in a room at the back. In spite of the weather several cars were pulled up outside the main door and there was a crowd inside. People stopping off on their way home to pick up a supper.

Inside, Mrs Chai, who Meg knew well, was busily scribbling orders on a pad and passing them through a hatch behind her to her husband. He worked in the kitchen with another cook. He was much older than his wife and spoke very little English.

Meg went through to the room at the back. The half-dozen tables were empty except for one, where a solitary boy sat reading a comic.

He looked up as Meg came in. ''Lo, Meg.'

'Hello, Melvin,' Meg answered.

Melvin Chai politely folded up his comic and came over. 'You after some supper for yourself and Mr Pennyquick?'

Meg smiled. 'Not tonight, Melvin. I came looking for Grandad himself actually. Isn't he supposed to be painting a dragon or something?'

Melvin swung round and pointed to the wall by the door. 'It's finished, see? Marvellous. Breathing flames and everything.'

Meg looked at the painting which had been done direct on to the shiny wall and had to admit it was one of Grandad's best.

'My Dad's real pleased,' Melvin said.

'When did Grandad finish it?' Meg asked.

'Just after dinnertime today. Earlier than he thought.'

Meg frowned. That meant that when she had seen Grandad's van outside the workshop earlier that afternoon, he had finished this job. So he must have gone on somewhere else, and where was anybody's guess.

'Was Davy with him?'

Melvin nodded. 'Oh yes, Davy was here all right. Sat and watched Mr Pennyquick with his mouth half open. You know what Davy's like with Dragons.' He looked at her strangely. 'Something wrong, Meg?'

'Not really,' said Meg. 'At least, I hope not. It's just that I thought they would be back by now. Grandad's not usually as late as this.'

Melvin gave her one of his famous grins, his eyes almost disappearing into his face. 'Tell you what, I'll come back to the workshop with you. Keep you company.'

He fetched his coat then got hold of her arm and pulled her towards the doors. His mother was still taking orders and would be for several hours yet. They served meals until late at night and Melvin was quite used to putting himself to bed in the cramped little flat where the three of them lived. Sometimes, in the summer, his mother and father did not get to bed until after midnight, then they would sleep on in the morning, leaving Melvin to make his own breakfast. In the holidays he often went up the hill to Meg's while she and her mother and grandfather were still having breakfast and Meg's mother would pull a chair up to the table for him to have a second meal.

So if Meg was worried or if there was some

problem about Mr Pennyquick, Melvin wanted to be there just in case he could help.

They stood in the doorway of the Take-Away and turned up their coat collars. 'Why don't we go and see if Davy's back yet?' Melvin suggested. 'It's not far from the workshop.'

'Yes, all right,' Meg said, slightly annoyed that she had not thought of it herself. What was the matter with her anyway? Her mind seemed to have turned into cotton wool.

Davy's mother was a large, red-faced woman, not the least like her son. At first she seemed bewildered by the arrival of the two children and Meg realized she had been expecting somebody else. She had a feeling she knew just who and her heart sank.

'I thought you were Davy,' the woman said, sounding cross about it. 'I've been expecting him this past hour.' She squinted in the darkness at the pair of them and recognized Melvin. 'He's not with you, I suppose?'

'No,' began Melvin but got no chance to continue.

'No, I thought not. He's with Mr Pennyquick I'm sure.' The woman stopped abruptly and stared at Meg.

Melvin took the opportunity and spoke. 'This is Meg, she's Mr Pennyquick's granddaughter. We had better be getting back to the workshop. They might both be there by now.'

With that he bustled Meg out into the rain, promising Davy's mother he would send her son home straight away if he was there.

He chattered all the way back up to the workshop seeing Meg's gloomy face: talked about the customer who dropped his meal of Chop Suey all over the floor as he hurried out of the Take-Away earlier that evening: told of Mr Ling, the other cook, whose English was so bad that he often said rude words without actually realizing they were rude. In fact Melvin worked hard for a smile and by the time they reached the yard Meg was actually laughing.

Her smile disappeared, however, when she saw the van was not back and the workshop still in darkness as she had left it.

.5

In the end, Davy managed to crawl back to the funfair on his hands and knees and sat inside the door shivering. He shut his eyes blotting every-

thing out – everything except his thoughts which would not go away.

What now? Sit and wait? It might be hours before anybody thought to wonder if there was someone on the pier. The seafront had been deserted earlier. Anyway, who would know, unless they happened to see the funfair lights?

The lights . . .

Davy looked up at the high ceiling where they blazed above him. He looked outside the blue doors where the first few yards of the pier were illuminated. He looked beyond to the lights of the town. Cheerful orange blobs lighting up warm, dry, *safe* little houses where people sat eating their suppers, or feet up in front of the fire watching the telly, all shuddering at the sound of the storm outside. He could see all the lights.

His mind turned the thought over and examined the other side of it. If he could see their lights from here, the lights of the funfair *could be seen from there*. What if he opened the doors wide and switched the lights on and off, like a signal?

Like Morse code. Except he did not know any Morse. But still, switching them on and off might be enough.

Where had Mr Pennyquick switched them on? Somewhere by the door, a cupboard full of switches and things. He ran across and tugged the cupboard door open.

There it was. A square metal box with a handle at the side. Mr Pennyquick had pulled the handle down to switch on, so if he were to push the handle up . . .

The building went black so suddenly it frightened him and he quickly pulled the handle back down. He found he was shaking and had to sit on the floor. After a while, he stood up and opened the blue doors, opened them wide, letting all the light spill out on to the pier.

The rain was still lashing down and he could see waves lapping the rails at the side of the pier, but the light was not enough to see as far as the damaged area.

Davy hurried back to the cupboard. He pushed the handle back up, plunging every-

thing into darkness again, waited a few seconds, then pulled it back down again. He did it six times then went back to the door.

Just what he expected to see, Davy was not sure. Certainly not anybody rushing up the pier, that would be too much to hope for. An answering light from the town? That seemed even less likely.

After a while, he went back to the cupboard and tried again ... and again ... and again ...

He blinked in the bright light. It wasn't going to work. It was plain useless. He slumped away from the cupboard fighting back more tears. Forcing himself, he walked over to Mr Penny-quick. The old man lay in exactly the same position breathing jerkily.

Suddenly there was another huge crash outside the open doors as a wave pounded the pier. Davy heard the same horrible creaking and splintering noise and knew that more of the pier had been washed into the sea. He began to shake again. Would the whole pier collapse soon? Would they be washed out to sea?

No matter how scary the darkness, how dangerous the journey, Davy knew he had to go for help before it was too late.

It was a nightmare walk. Waves swept about him, salting his lips and eyes and soaking his already wet clothes until he was numb with cold. The wooden rail in his hands and the few yards of dark slimy floor which he could manage to see ahead of him were his only thoughts. He counted his steps to shut out the danger from his mind. It was an old game his father used to play when he had been small and grown tired of walking home.

'Count the steps, Davy. Eat them up one at a time.'

And so Davy ate each slippery step along the pier. Thirty-one, thirty-two, thirty-three . . .

Back at the workshop, Meg had been standing by the window, staring at her own reflection in the glass. The window had been turned into a mirror by the workshop light and the darkness outside.

'Something must have happened,' she said.

'The van must have broken down or something – something worse.'

Melvin was about to answer when the telephone rang. It was on a shelf by the door and Meg ran across to pick up the receiver. Her hand was shaking and so was her voice.

'He – hello?'

'Hello? Is that Mr Pennyquick – no, I can hear it isn't. I have dialled the right number, haven't I?' It was a man's voice, very snappy.

Meg swallowed and tried to explain. 'This is Mr Pennyquick's workshop, Mellisea 6929. I'm afraid Mr Pennyquick is out –'

'Well when he comes back, kindly tell him Mr Bragg called. Tell him I am most anxious to know when the pier job will be finished and, if he hasn't already begun, to start tomorrow without fail.'

Meg held the receiver a few inches from her ear as the scratchy voice rambled on. Melvin could hear as well and he screwed up a face. Eventually Mr Bragg's battery ran down and

Meg just had time to say 'Good-bye' before he slammed down the phone.

'Him and his precious pier,' said Melvin, but Meg was not listening. She had walked over to the window again, frowning as she peered out.

'Switch off the light, Melv.'

'Eh?' said Melvin, but did as she asked.

The mirror vanished and Meg could see across the rooftops to the sea. She beckoned to Melvin. 'Quick. Out there.'

Melvin could see nothing but darkness and the lights from the houses farther round the bay.

'It's gone,' Meg said surprised. 'I thought I saw a light – on the pier.' Melvin stared at her. 'There!' she went on. 'There it is again!'

They both watched in silence. A few seconds later the light went out . . . then came on again.

A niggling little thought edged its way into Meg's brain. 'It must be Grandad.' Her voice sounded as though it belonged to somebody else.

Melvin was still watching the light. 'It's almost like some sort of signal.'

Without another word they hurried out to the

stairway and the rain. Running down the tiny alleyways, they lost sight of the pier. The street-lights splashed pools of light every few yards and, in them, they glimpsed each other's faces, wide-eyed and anxious.

At the boathouse on the corner they were able to see the pier again.

'The light's stopped flashing,' Meg said. 'There! There's Grandad's van.'

It stood under the streetlight on the slope opposite the pier gates and, as they ran across, the waves pounded up the beach and slapped against the sea wall.

'He never locks it,' Meg said as she pulled open the driver's door. 'Mum's always telling him about it.'

They ran down to the pier and pulled open the gates at the end. The darkness and the noise halted them and Meg gripped Melvin's arm. Between them and the funfair lights was a black nothingness.

'If only we had brought a torch,' Melvin said. 'Grandad will have his with him.'

'We'll just have to go in the dark then. At least, I will.'

'I'm not staying here on my own,' said Meg. 'If you go, so do I.'

Melvin could see there was going to be no arguing with her. She turned round and stared at the van then pulled Melvin's arm.

'C'mon.'

'What –'

'The van. We're going to use the van, or at least its headlights.'

Melvin still did not see.

'To light up the pier.' Meg climbed in behind the steering wheel and bent over to sort out the pedals.

'Meg! You sure –?'

''Course I'm sure,' said Meg with more confidence than she felt. 'I've watched Grandad millions of times. Anyway, we don't have to start the engine because there's a slope. All I have to do is let the handbrake off and steer the van down to the pier. You go round the back and give me a push when I shout.'

So Melvin put his hands against the back doors and when Meg shouted 'Right' he gave it a shove. Then he watched from behind as the little van trundled down the slope, at first bumping the pavement but then keeping a remarkably straight course down to the pier. Meg nosed it up to the gates before stopping jerkily.

Melvin ran down behind and reached her

just as she found the headlight switch and flooded the pier with light. They both gasped at what they saw in front of them.

Some distance from the gates a gaping hole in the pier flooring stretched more than half-way across. The rail on the damaged side was ripped away and broken floorboards stuck up like broken fingernails. Every so often a wave burst up through the hole and took back a bit more flooring with it.

Then they saw Davy. He was just the other side of the wreckage clinging to the rail. His white face was screwed up against the sudden glare of the headlights.

.6

Davy stood quite still until Meg and Melvin reached him, then he motioned with his head towards the funfair and as the three of them went back he told them what had happened.

The first thing Davy noticed was that Mr Pennyquick had moved slightly and he ran across. The old man blinked up at him and gave a faint smile. 'What's happening?' he asked as the other two arrived at Davy's side.

Meg told him, slowly, carefully, and without mentioning the damaged pier. She told how Davy had been struggling back in the darkness and how they had lit up the pier with the van's headlights.

Mr Pennyquick twinkled, 'Well done.' Then he closed his eyes against the pain in his feet. At

that moment there was another crash outside as more of the pier collapsed. Mr Pennyquick looked up. 'What's that?'

The three of them looked at one another then Meg told him.

'You must all go back,' Mr Pennyquick said after Meg had finished.

'No,' Davy said firmly. 'Not without you.'

Meg was startled. She had never seen Davy so determined.

'Davy lad, I can't even get on my feet,' said Mr Pennyquick.

'I know,' said Davy, 'but I've been thinking. There's the Treasure Trail Train.' He pointed to the row of brightly coloured trucks by the wall.

Melvin understood quickly. 'But there's no engine.'

'We don't need one,' said Davy, and he ran over and rolled one of the trucks back. The wheels, freshly oiled ready for the Easter holiday, turned easily.

Mr Pennyquick stared at Davy. 'I've always

said there was more to you than met the eye, Davy. You've proved me right today.'

Although Mr Pennyquick was able to help by pulling himself up with his arms and steadying himself as they guided him into the narrow seat of the truck, his face turned grey and he almost passed out again.

A dragon's head was moulded on to the front of the truck and Davy pulled this while Meg and Melvin pushed from behind. They slowly made their way forwards, first to the doors then out into the storm..The pier, spotlit by the van's headlights, was like one of Davy's pictures come to life. Several times huge clouds of foam burst up through the wrecked floor spraying the rescue group and claiming more of the wooden boards. Soon the funfair end would be completely cut off from the shore. Urgently, their heads bent against the wind, the children fought their way back with their injured passenger.

As the dragon truck finally bumped to a halt beside the van, Davy turned just in time to see the pier split into two halves by the furious sea.

Afterwards, whenever Davy thought about that night, the last clear picture in his mind was the pier breaking in two. What followed was just a jumble. Was it Meg that had gone to telephone for help? Or was it Melvin? Anyway, the ambulance had arrived at some stage and

whisked Mr Pennyquick away. Davy had a hazy picture of Meg climbing into the ambulance with her grandfather. The next thing he could remember was sitting in the back of his father's car with Melvin, and Melvin telling what had happened. He must have dropped off to sleep about then for he could not remember hearing Melvin finish.

The next day he was in bed with a cold, which made him cross because he had wanted to go and see Mr Pennyquick. However, Meg and Melvin arrived later on with the news that the old man had not broken any bones in the fall, just badly sprained both ankles.

'He won't be able to work for a while,' Meg said, 'but Mum says the rest will do him good.'

Then, for the next half-hour, she and Melvin sat on the edge of Davy's bed and chattered excitedly about the previous night's happenings and how brave Davy had been. Davy said very little but grinned happily at his two friends – for that was what they were now, of that he was sure. But as they talked on, Davy's mind

wandered off. He began to think about a picture. A picture of a huge sea leaping into the sky around a tiny, broken old pier. Eyes and faces staring blearily through the darkness and a jagged spear of lightning splitting the sky in an orange glare. And large bony fingers poking up through the gaping floor, waiting to curl around the small, bent figure crawling along the slimy boards . . .